He gave his second son the donkey.

He gave his third son the cat.

The third son was sad.

He had no money.

How could he look after a cat?

3

"Don't be sad, Master," said Puss.

"You can talk!" said the miller's son.

"Yes," said Puss. "I have a clever plan.

But first I need some boots."

The miller's son got Puss some boots

and a hat.

"For my plan to work," Puss said,

"you must pretend to be

the Marquis of Carrabas."

# Puss in Boots

by Jill Atkins and Shahab Shamshirsaz

W

Once, there was an old miller
with three sons. Before he died,
the miller gave each son one thing.
He gave his first son the mill.

Next day, Puss took some rabbits to
the king's palace. He bowed to the king.
"These are a present from my master,
the Marquis of Carrabas," said Puss.
The king was pleased.

Every day, Puss took presents to the palace. "From the Marquis of Carrabas," he said.

One day, Puss heard some news.
The king and the princess would soon
be passing by.
"Quick," said Puss. "Get in the river."
The miller's son took off his clothes
and dived in. Puss hid the clothes.

"Help!" cried Puss. "Robbers have stolen my master's clothes."

The king sent servants to fetch some new clothes. The miller's son put them on. He looked like a real marquis!

"Come, Marquis," said the king.

"Ride in my coach."

When the miller's son and the princess

saw each other, they fell in love.

"But I am too poor to marry

a princess," thought the miller's son.

Puss ran ahead. He saw some farmers.
He told them, "If the king asks you
who owns these fields, you must say
the Marquis of Carrabas."

Soon, the coach came along.

The king asked the farmers,

"Who owns these fields?"

"The Marquis of Carrabas,"

replied the farmers.

"Is that your master's castle?" the king asked Puss. "I would like to visit it."

"Of course," said Puss. "I'll go and get everything ready."

The castle belonged to a mean giant.

Puss had a plan to trick him.

"What do you want?" roared the giant.

"Is it true that you can turn into

different animals?" asked Puss.

"Yes," replied the giant.

And he turned into a lion.

"Very clever," said Puss.

"But can you turn into a mouse?"

"Yes," replied the giant.

And he turned into a mouse.

Puss gobbled him up.

Just then, the coach arrived.

The miller's son led the king

and the princess into the castle.

"What a beautiful castle," said the king.

"You must be very rich."

The princess and the miller's son smiled at each other.

Very soon, they were married.

And they all lived happily ever after, especially Puss.

# Story order

Look at these 5 pictures and captions.
Put the pictures in the right order
to retell the story.

1

Puss took presents to the palace.

2

The miller's son and the princess
were married.

**3**

The miller's son got some boots for Puss.

**4**

The miller's son jumped in the river.

**5**

Puss told the giant to turn into a mouse.

# Guide for Independent Reading

This series is designed to provide an opportunity for your child to read on their own. These notes are written for you to help your child choose a book and to read it independently.

In school, your child's teacher will often be using reading books which have been banded to support the process of learning to read. Use the book band colour your child is reading in school to help you make a good choice. *Puss in Boots* is a good choice for children reading at Turquoise Band in their classroom to read independently.

The aim of independent reading is to read this book with ease, so that your child enjoys the story and relates it to their own experiences.

## About the book

The miller's son is very poor, but he does own a very special cat. Puss is determined to be rich, and he has a plan.

## Before reading

Help your child to learn how to make good choices by asking:

"Why did you choose this book? Why do you think you will enjoy it?" Look at the cover together and ask: "What do you think the story will be about?" Ask your child to think of what they already know about the story context. Then ask your child to read the title aloud.

Ask: "Do you think the cat in this story is going to be special in some way? If so, what do you think might be special about him?"

Remind your child that they can sound out a word in syllable chunks if they get stuck. Decide together whether your child will read the story independently or read it aloud to you.